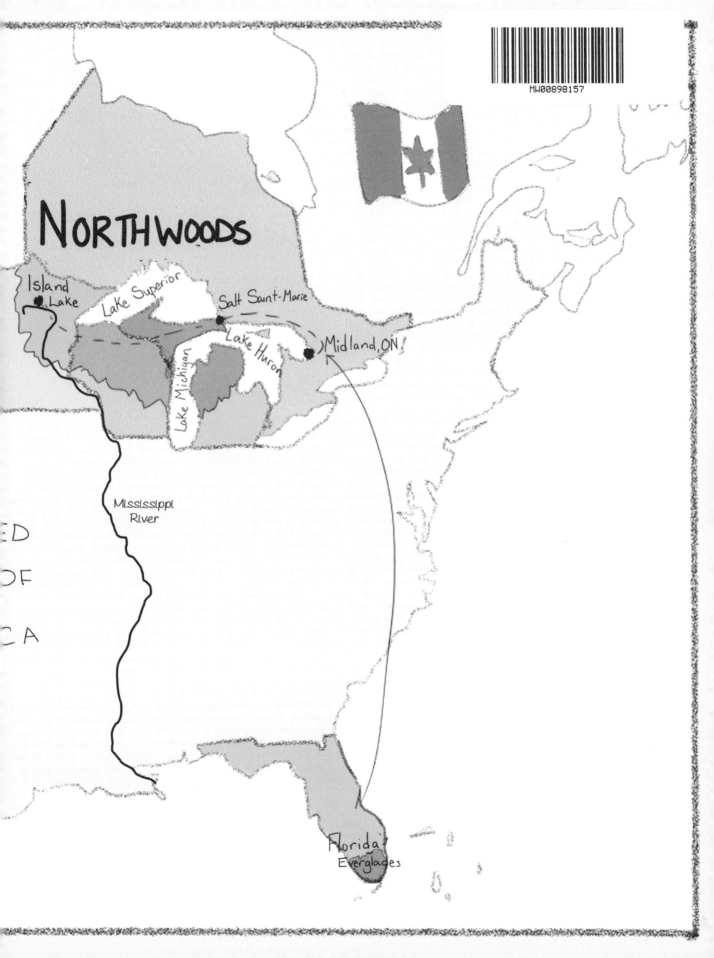

NORTHWOODS

Island Lake

Lake Superior

Salt Saint-Marie

Lake Michigan

Lake Huron

Midland, ON

Mississippi River

ED

OF

CA

Florida Everglades

A big thank you to Bill and Doris Eriksen
for introducing us to Island Lake and to Len and
Norma Jean Grotnes and family at Valhalla Resort.

www.mascotbooks.com

Barlow Explores the Northwoods

For more information, please contact:
Mascot Books
620 Herndon Parkway #320
Herndon, VA 20170
info@mascotbooks.com

Library of Congress Control Number: 2020900302

CPSIA Code: PRT0320A
ISBN-13: 978-1-64543-347-7

Printed in the United States

BARLOW
Explores the Northwoods

William Ericksen and Lanny Scholes-Ericksen
illustrated by Alaina Luise

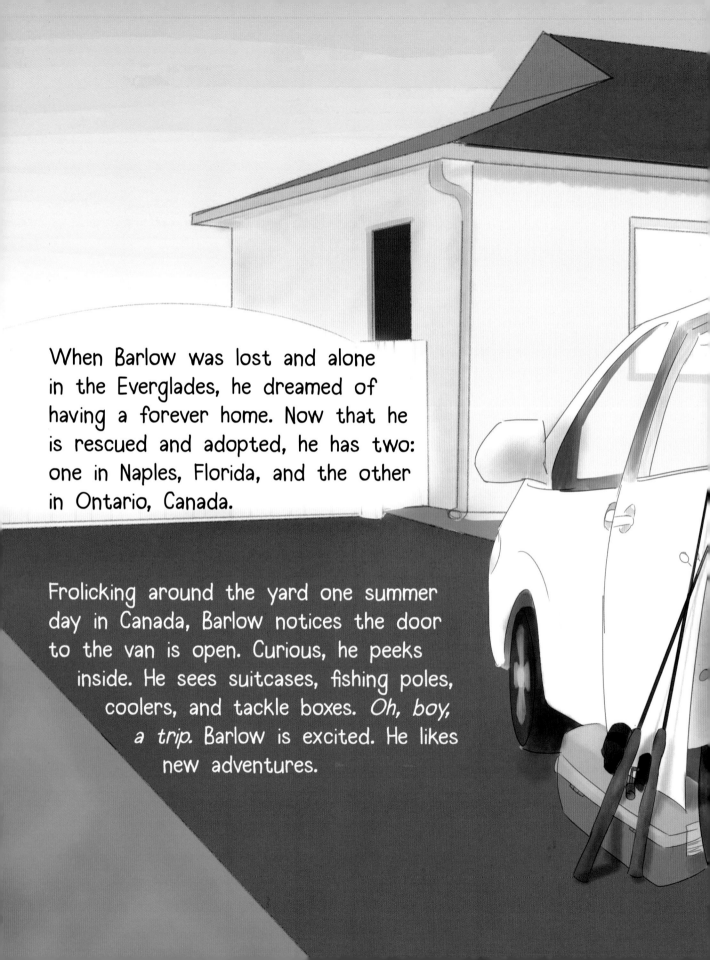

When Barlow was lost and alone in the Everglades, he dreamed of having a forever home. Now that he is rescued and adopted, he has two: one in Naples, Florida, and the other in Ontario, Canada.

Frolicking around the yard one summer day in Canada, Barlow notices the door to the van is open. Curious, he peeks inside. He sees suitcases, fishing poles, coolers, and tackle boxes. *Oh, boy, a trip.* Barlow is excited. He likes new adventures.

Barlow's owners do not have to call him when they are ready to leave. He is already in the backseat waiting for them. As the van travels down the highway toward the Northwoods of Minnesota in the United States, Barlow grows tired after a time. He curls up on his favorite blanket and falls fast asleep.

Many miles later, Barlow wakes up just in time to see a horse-drawn buggy at the side of the road and a bearded man in a straw hat standing next to it.

The lady at his side wears a long dress and a white bonnet. They are Mennonite farmers. They brought vegetables, fruit, and handmade quilts from their farm to the roadside stand in the buggy because they do not drive cars or tractors. While his owners buy vegetables, Barlow eyes the horse. It is huge! He is careful not to get too close.

The next stop is a marina filled with boats next to a park and the border crossing into the United States from Canada.

When Barlow sees the agent in the booth, his mouth waters. He thinks, *Oh goodie, a treat.* He pokes his head out of the window to be ready. The agent laughs. "Sorry, puppy, this is not a drive-through restaurant," he says. "No treats here."

After two nights in a motel and three days on the road, Barlow and his family arrive at the Valhalla Resort on Island Lake in Minnesota. Barlow leans out of the window to look around. In front of the resort's manor house, two young deer stop nibbling the grass to look at him.

Barlow wants to play, but the van keeps going down a tree-covered road to a log cabin on the edge of a beach. Finally, the van door opens. Barlow jumps out to explore around the cabin.

In the evening, Barlow stretches out next to the campfire. He listens to the cries of loons and the hoot of an owl in a nearby tree. When his nose smells toasted marshmallows, Barlow sits on his hind legs and begs with his paws. The treats are too hot to eat. No matter, he is having an excellent time.

At bedtime, Barlow waits
in the cabin while his
owners douse the campfire
and clean up. He stands on his hind legs to look
out the window. Something fast,
furry, and squeaky scurries over his paws
and across the floor. *Eek! What was that?*
Frightened and shaking, he hides under the bed.

The next morning, Barlow boards a small motor boat to go across Island Lake to Eagle Bay. He wears his bright yellow lifejacket and sits in the bow. The rest of the world is still asleep. Only the boat motor and the loons disturb the quiet. When the sun rises, it makes mist rise from the lake water. Barlow thinks it is a beautiful sight.

At Eagle Bay, Barlow sees two eaglets sharing a nest high in a pine tree. Eager for breakfast, they look on as their mother swoops low over the water to catch fish. Not far from the boat, a family of four loons scour the water for their breakfast. One of the baby loons rides on its mother's back. *What fun,* Barlow thinks.

Barlow is eager to return to the beach after his boat trip. He likes playing in the sand with the children. His Labrador retriever friends, Sonny and Gus, are there, too. Before long, the dogs are jumping, running, and chasing each other. When Sonny and Gus charge into the lake, Barlow screeches to a stop at the edge of the water. He does not like wet paws.

At the end of a long, exciting day, Barlow is tired. In the cabin, he falls asleep dreaming of marshmallows.

The following morning, Barlow goes for a walk. As he sniffs his way down the road, he discovers a pond hidden behind long reeds and tall cattails. It is called Lily Pad Bay because of many white and yellow flowered lily pads that float on the surface of the water. They are so close together that Barlow does not notice the water underneath them. When a duck flies by, he chases it right off the dock. Splash! What a surprise!

On the other side of the pond, Barlow sees a beaver building a lodge. Barlow also puts his nose too close to a crayfish creeping along the path. *Ouch!*

In the afternoon, Barlow and his family take a boat ride around Round Island. On the way, they stop to help a family whose boat is out of gas. Barlow's boat pulls the stranded boaters back to shore with a rope. Barlow is a hero!

The next day, Barlow and his family drive to Park Rapids, Minnesota to shop and have lunch. Later in the day, they head to Itasca State Park to see the beginning of the Mississippi River, the second-longest river in the United States.

At the park, Barlow wades in the shallow headwaters with the kids and other dogs. He does not mind his wet paws. It is a hot day; the water feels cool on his paws.

When the van returns to the cabin on the shore of the lake, it is dark except for the bright quarter moon shining in the sky. Barlow yawns, stretches, and jumps out of the van. Inside the cabin, he stomps in circles on top of his bed, all the while thinking about his adventures at Island Lake. When his bed is just right, he plops down and curls up. His last thought before falling asleep is: *I hope we come back next year.*

Acknowledgments from Lanny and Bill

Once again, we would like to thank our friends Pat Brun and Leni Edwards for their invaluable assistance in the development of this book. In addition, we thank our illustrator, Alaina Luise, who has captured Barlow's personality and the story so incredibly well.

This is a picture of Barlow, Lanny, and Bill at a book signing. We want to thank all those who work in animal shelters. Without them, Barlow would not have been united with us. We hope our stories encourage others to rescue lost and abandoned dogs. Even dogs have angels.

CANADA

THE U
STAT
AM

MEXICO